Ted's
Bike Ride

Ted's Bike Ride

by Tom & Nikki Hart

illustrated by Andreea Togoe

Dear Roseanna,

This is Ted. He was knitted by Granny and
inspired us to write this book for you.
We hope you like it!

With lots of love,
Mummy & Daddy

xxx

Ted found a bike and away he rode,
Peddling quickly down the road

Over the hill as quick as can be,
"What's that in the distance I can see?"

1

Ted peddled faster and mopped his brow,
"Oh now I see, it's a black and white cow."

"Hello Mrs. Cow and how do you do?
Are you able to teach me anything new?"

"Hello Ted and good morning to you,
All I can teach you is how to Moo.

Moooooo

mooO

MooO

Mooooool

Moooood mooo

"Thank you Mrs. Cow, now I really must run,
But I will Moo all day as it's so much fun!"

5

Ted peddled on and passed a huge log,
Mooing out loudly before spotting a dog.

"Hello Mr. Dog and how do you do?
Are you able to teach me anything new?"

"Hello Ted, you look out of puff,
All I can teach you is how to Woof.

Woof

Woof

Woof

Woof

Woof

Woof

Woof

8

"Thank you Mr. Dog, now I really must run,
But I will Woof all day as it's so much fun!"

9

Off Ted went going past a golf course,
Woofing out loudly when he spotted a horse.

"Hello Mr. Horse and how do you do?
Are you able to teach me anything new?"

"Hello Ted, have you had a good day?
All I can teach you is how to Neigh.

11

neeeigh

neeeigh

neeeeigh

neeeigh

neeeigh

12

neeeigh neeeigh

neeeigh

Back on his bike Ted set off again,
Peddling faster as it started to rain.

13

Dashing for cover under a tree Ted hid,
Neighing out loudly when he spotted a pig.

"Hello Mr. Pig and how do you do?
Are you able to teach me anything new?"

"Hello Ted, I can't see the point,
All I can teach you is how to Oink.

Oink

Oink

Oink

"Thank you Mr. Pig, now I really must run,
But I will Oink all day as it's so much fun!"

Peddling quickly Ted set off again,
Splashing through puddles made by the rain.

17

Wearing his rain coat in case of bad luck,
Ted was Oinking out loudly when he spotted a duck.

"Hello Mr. Duck and how do you do?
Are you able to teach me anything new?"

"Hello Ted, I do like your Mac,
But all I can teach you is how to Quack.

20

"Thank you Mr. Duck, now I really must run,
But I will Quack all day as it's so much fun!"

21

Feeling quite hungry and needing a sleep,
Ted Quacked as he rode, then he spotted a sheep.

"Hello Mrs. Sheep and how do you do?
Are you able to teach me anything new?"

"Hello Ted, have you come far?
All I can teach you is how to Baa.

"Thank you Mrs. Sheep now I really must run,
But I will Baa all day as it's so much fun!"

Ted was rather tired as he set off for home,
He mooed and he woofed as he got in the zone.

He neighed and he oinked as he went on his way,
And he quacked and he baa'd as he sped past the hay.

When he got home he wiped his feet on the mat,
Went into the kitchen and spotted his cat.

26

"Hello Mr. Cat and how do you do?
Are you able to teach me anything new?"

Mr. Cat didn't move or welcome Ted home,
He looked down his nose and gave out a moan.

28

"Oh Ted, you are welcome to give me a stroke,
But asking for help is a bit of a joke."

And with that the cat turned saying that's all for now
But as he curled up he whispered…

Meeooow

Printed in Great Britain
by Amazon